For David, with love
~KW

For Cassie
~VC

Copyright © 2004 by Good Books, Intercourse, PA 17534
International Standard Book Number: 1-56148-446-6

Library of Congress Catalog Card Number: 2004004173

Text copyright © Kathryn White 2004
Illustrations copyright © Vanessa Cabban 2004

Original edition published in English by Little Tiger Press, an imprint of
Magi Publications, London, England, 2004.
Printed in Belgium by Proost

Library of Congress Cataloging-in-Publication Data

White, Kathryn (Kathryn Ivy)
Nutty nut chase / Kathryn White ; illustrated by Vanessa Cabban.
p. cm.
"Original edition published in English by Little Tiger Press, an imprint of
Magi Publications, London, England, 2004."
Summary: When a shiny brown nut pops out of the ground, each animal
wants it for him or herself, but the extraordinary nut turns out to be the source
of a delicious treat for everyone.
ISBN 1-56148-446-6 (hardcover)
[1. Nuts--Fiction. 2. Animals--Fiction.] I. Cabban, Vanessa, 1971- ill. II. Title.
PZ7.W58376Nu 2004
[E]--dc22
2004004173

The Nutty Nut Chase

Kathryn White   *Illustrated by* Vanessa Cabban

Good Books

Intercourse, PA 17534

800/762-7171

www.goodbks.com

Hickory was making rude faces at Pecan
when the strangest thing happened.

POP!

A shiny brown nut suddenly burst up from the ground. It wobbled and shook, wibbled and quivered, then lay there, teasingly delicious.

"Wow, lunch!" Pecan shouted.
"Wow, lunch and dinner!" Hickory screeched.
"It's my nut," said Pecan.
"It's mine," snapped Hickory.

"Who's making that noise?" shouted Badger.
"I'm trying to sleep."
All the animals came out to see what was happening.

"My nut!" Pecan shouted.

"It's mine!" yelled Hickory. "I saw it first."

"Did not."

"Did so."

"Box his ears!" shouted Littlest Rabbit.

"Certainly not. Boxing ears doesn't solve problems," said Badger firmly.

"Oh," said Littlest Rabbit, disappointed, "then bop his nose."

"No boxing or bopping," said Badger. "There will be a competition and the winner will get the nut."

"I know," said Hedgehog. "The prickliest wins the nut."
"But you're the prickliest," said Pecan and Hickory.
"So I am!" said Hedgehog, delighted. "I win! I get the nut."
"Cuddliest gets the nut," said Littlest Rabbit, "I win!"

"Enough!"

said Badger. "We will have a
race. First to reach the post wins."
"Hooray, a race!" everyone cheered.

Blackbird whistled the
start of the race. They were off.
Pecan and Hickory shot ahead
but the rabbits were close behind.
Hedgehog tried to run but only managed
a waddle. In a huff, he curled himself into
a ball and rolled full speed down the slope.
    Littlest Rabbit looked back to see a prickly
ball spinning towards them. "Look out!"
he called. Too late!

Hedgehog crashed through the racers like a cannonball and everyone landed in a prickly heap.

"Oh dear," tutted Badger. "We'll have to start again. And prickly cannonballs aren't allowed."

Hedgehog snorted
and sulked off.

Blackbird whistled and they were off again.
Pecan and Hickory were neck and neck.
"My nut!" shouted Pecan triumphantly. "I win!"
"No!" shouted Hickory. "It's mine! I win!"

Suddenly the nut began to move. It twitched
and jerked, joggled and jiggled until PLOP!
It disappeared down under the ground.
  "It's a magic nut!" shouted Littlest Rabbit.
  "Nutty magic!" squealed Hedgehog, racing back to see.
  "Bet it would have tasted magic too," said Shrew.

POP!
The nut sprang up
right in front of Shrew.
 "Quick, grab it!" shouted Littlest Rabbit.
  All the animals shot across the grass, rolling and shrieking,
   jumping and hopping, banging and bopping into each other.
 "I've got it!" shouted Hedgehog, but the nut vanished again.
 "That's my nose!" Shrew squeaked.

"Shhhhh!" said Badger suddenly. "Look."

He pointed at the magic nut that had appeared at his feet. Everyone tiptoed up to it. The nut shook and quivered. The animals looked in amazement.

"Help!" squealed the nut.

"AAAH!" shrieked Littlest Rabbit. "A talking nut."

"You're a talking nut," said Pecan.

Pecan and Hickory bent down and pulled and tugged, yanked and wrenched at the nutshell with all their might.

POP!

Out flew the nutshell, sending Pecan and Hickory rolling backwards. And there, where the nut had been, was Mole!

Mole shook himself and stood up on his two tiny legs. "Thanks!" he said. "I thought I would be stuck in that nutshell forever."

Littlest Rabbit put the empty shell on his head. "It makes a great hat," he giggled.

"That looked like the tastiest nut ever," groaned Pecan and Hickory.

"There's plenty more where that came from," chirped Mole and he disappeared underground.

Suddenly shiny nuts began popping up all over the place.
"There's enough for everyone," Mole chuckled.

POP! POP!

POP!

"Magic!" shouted Hickory.
"Magic!" shouted Pecan.
"Nutty magic!" everyone
shouted, and they all
munched with delight.

POP!